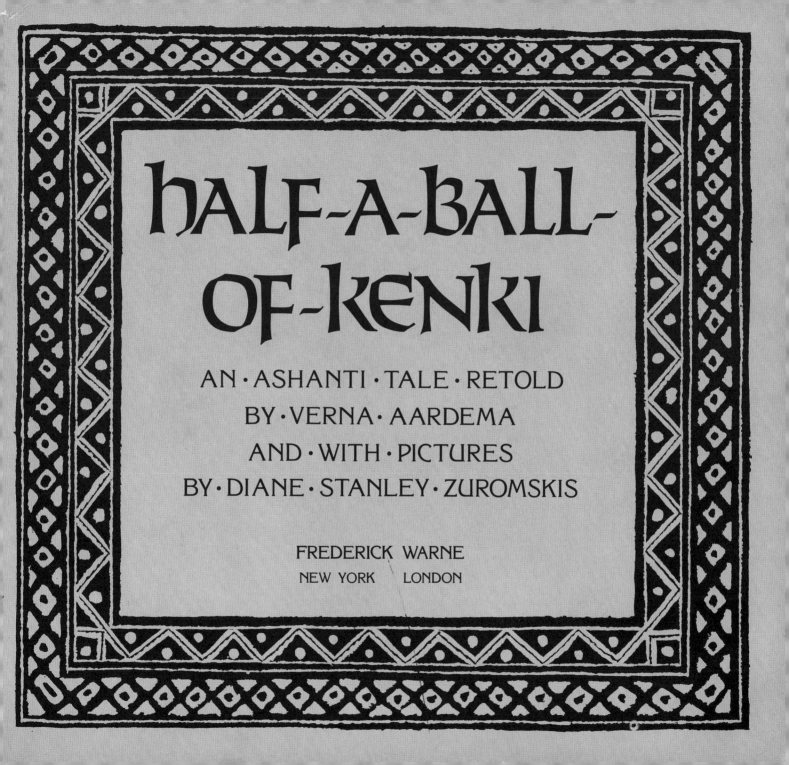

HALF-A-BALL-OF-KENKI

AN · ASHANTI · TALE · RETOLD
BY · VERNA · AARDEMA
AND · WITH · PICTURES
BY · DIANE · STANLEY · ZUROMSKIS

FREDERICK WARNE

NEW YORK   LONDON

For my niece in California, Maya Ann Agaskar
V.A.

For my Mother
D.S.Z.

Adapted from Akan-Ashanti Folk-Tales by R. S. Rattray (1930)
pp. 20-27 by permission of Oxford University Press.

Frederick Warne & Co., Inc. New York, New York

Designed by Diane Stanley Zuromskis
Printed in the United States of America by A. Hoen & Co.

1 2 3 4 5 82 81 80 79

Library of Congress Cataloging in Publication Data
Aardema, Verna.
Half-a-ball-of-kenki.
Summary: Half-a-Ball-of-Kenki rescues Fly
from Leopard and in the ensuing fray, Leopard
receives a spotted coat forever.
[1. Folklore, Ashanti] I. Title.
PZ8.1.A213Hal [398.2] [E] 78-16135
ISBN 0-7232-6158-X

The Ashanti storyteller says: I do not mean, I do not really mean that this story is true.

**L**ONG AGO AND FAR AWAY, FLY AND LEOPARD were friends. One day Leopard said, "Fly, let's go looking for girls to marry."

"Yo!" cried Fly. "That will be fun for me. The girls will like me better than you."

"**Kye, kye, kye**," laughed Leopard. "We shall see!" Then he bathed and oiled his fur. And he put a gold chain around his neck, and anklets with bells of gold on his front feet. To make sure his friend did not outshine him, he tied up his dirty old sleeping mat and gave it to Fly to carry on his head.

The two set out down the path, the gold bells singing **gben, gben, gben** as they walked along.

Presently, they came to a village. Fly entered first. He put down his burden and said to the people in the plaza, "Mothers all and fathers all, I give you morning greetings."

The people greeted him in return, and the young maids gathered about him.

Then Leopard swaggered through the gate, jingling his anklets
with every step **gben, gben, gben**! He smiled a crafty smile and said,
"Mothers all and fathers all . . ."

But the chief cried, "Off with you!
How dare you enter our village!" He said,
"**Sah**!" to his dog. And the dog bolted
after Leopard. Leopard went flying
kuputu, kuputu, kuputu
out the gate!

Fly followed him out. And the two went on. At length, they
arrived at another town.

Again, Fly entered first. The people greeted him, and the young girls clustered around him.

But when Leopard arrived, he was driven off just as before.

Back on the path Leopard said, "Look here, Fly! Give me that old mat. And you take these gold things and adorn yourself. If it is because of that mat that the girls love you, we shall see!"

So Fly put on the gold ornaments, Leopard carried the mat, and they went on their way.

When they reached the next village, Leopard entered first, with the dirty old mat on his head. He said, "Mothers all and fathers all, I give you midday greetings."

But the women and children screamed and ran **pamdal** into their houses. And the men grabbed their spears! Leopard scuttled away so fast that the mat fell off his head.

A small time later Leopard watched through a crack in the fence as Fly entered the plaza and was welcomed by the people. Leopard heard a maiden say, **"Tih, tih**! How handsome you look with those gold things on. If it were not for the beating I would get, I would go away with you."

Leopard turned away in disgust.

He said, "When the moon is out, the stars are dim. And I can't go looking for girls with a handsome man like him!"

When Fly joined Leopard on the path, Leopard was overcome with jealousy. He cried, "Stand still, Fly! Take off those gold things and give them to me quickly, quickly, quickly!"

As Fly was slipping them off, Leopard plucked a long creeper. He grabbed hold of Fly and bound him to a palm tree—winding the creeper **kpong, kpong, kpong**. Then he hid himself nearby.

Presently, Nkatee, the Peanut, came down the path
on her way to market. She was stepping daintily
pip, pip, pip over the roots that crisscrossed
the path. She saw the bundle on the tree
and asked, "Who is hanging there so very black?
Who is hanging there so very glossy?"

Fly sang:

> "It's I, the Fly, tied
> By Leopard to this tree,
> Because the girls hated him,
> But they loved me.
> Ooo! Please come and set me free!"

But Nkatee said, "If I set you free, Leopard will make peanut soup of me!" And she hurried off **pip-pip-pip-pip**, **pip-pip-pip**!

Soon Kwadu, the Banana, came striding
by **tuk-pik, tuk-pik**. She saw Fly
and asked, "Who is hanging there so very black?
Who is hanging there so very glossy?"
Fly sang:

> "It's I, the Fly, tied
> By Leopard to this tree,
> Because the girls hated him,
> But they loved me.
> Ooo! Please come and set me free!"

Kwadu said, "If I loosened you, Leopard would mash me to
fu-fu!" (Fu-fu is mashed banana.) And she hurried off
tuk-pik, tuk-pik, tuk-pik!

At last there came along Dokonfa, half a ball of kenki, which is cold cornmeal mush. Half-a-Ball-of-Kenki was singing:

"I'm Half-a-Ball-of-Kenki,
  Which is better than none.
  I'm Half-a-Ball-of-Kenki,
  And two of me makes one."

Then she saw Fly and asked, "Who is hanging there so very black? Who is hanging there so very glossy?"
Fly sang:

"It's I, the Fly, tied
  By Leopard to this tree,
  Because the girls hated him,
  But they loved me.
  Ooo! Please come and set me free!"

Half-a-Ball-of-Kenki said,
"I have heard you.
And I shall set you free!"
She unwound the creeper
kpung, kpung, kpung.

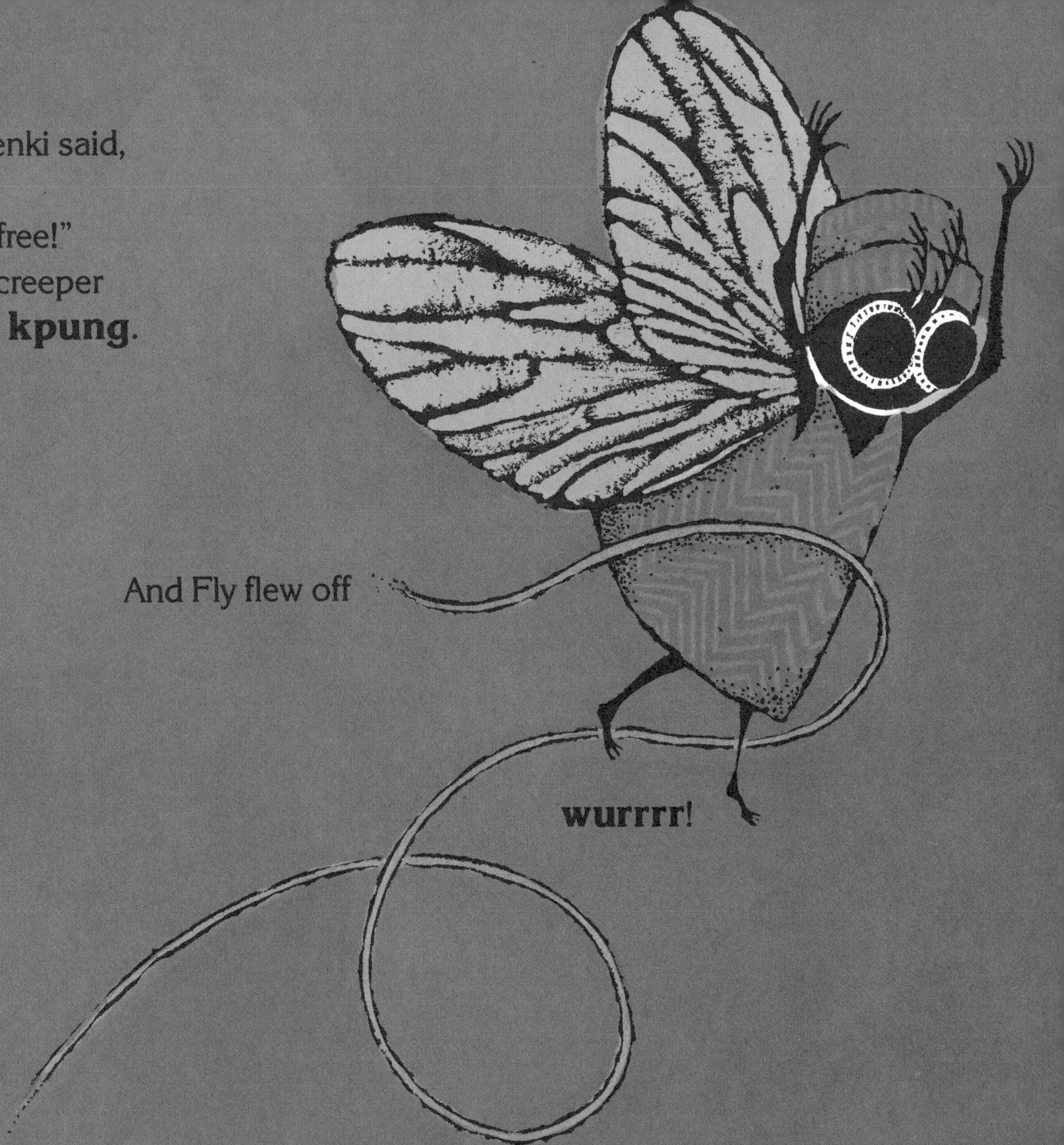

And Fly flew off

wurrrr!

Then Leopard leaped **harrr** out of the bushes! He bellowed,
"Why have you freed my man?"

"Well, I have done it," said Half-a-Ball-of-Kenki. "And what you
will do to me do!"

"You and I will fight," said Leopard.

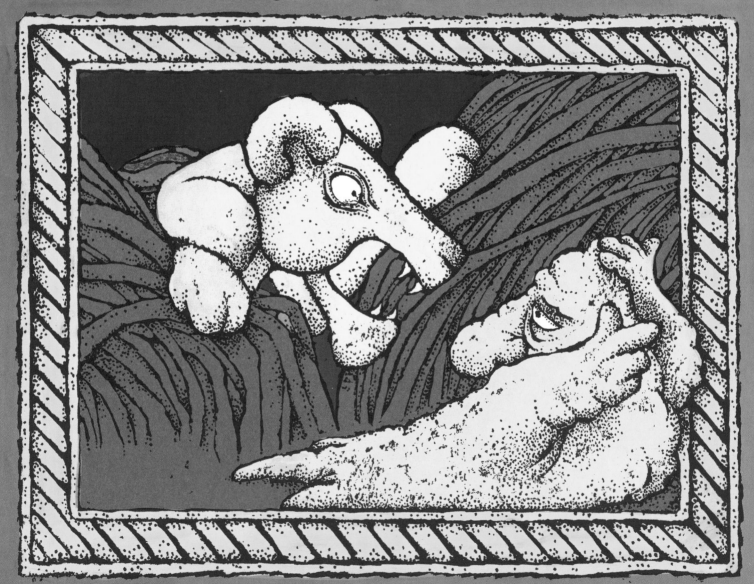

Half-a-Ball-of-Kenki said,
"It is already
early evening.
If we are going
to fight,
let us make
a fire first."
So they broke wood
and set it alight
in the middle
of the path.

Then they began to wrestle. Round and round they tumbled. And soon Leopard tore Half-a-Ball-of-Kenki from him and threw her **blim** against a tree!

"A thing like that is nothing," said Half-a-Ball-of-Kenki as she pulled herself together.

They fought again. And Leopard slammed Half-a-Ball-of-Kenki deep into the sand! **Ras, ras, ras** she dug herself out, and brushed herself off. Then she said, "Now, we'll really fight! That was just for practice."

They grappled again, rolling on the ground **dadwa, dadwa, dadwa**! Then suddenly Half-a-Ball-of-Kenki gathered all her strength, lifted up Leopard, and threw him **kabat** into the fire!

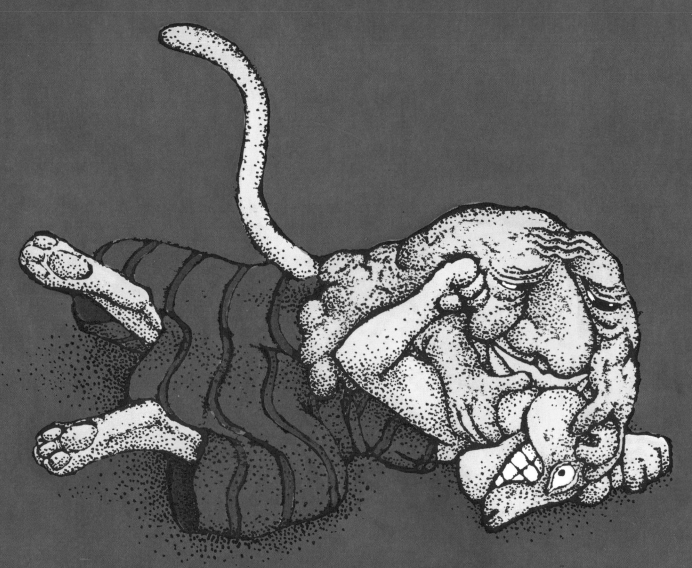

"I'm out! I'm out! I'm out!" cried Leopard.
And that is how the leopard got his cry.
When he came out of the fire, his body was
all spotted. There were black spots where the
charred wood had touched him. There were
white spots where the ashes had touched him.
And that is how the leopard got a spotted coat.

And to this day flies sit upon the leaves in which kenki has been wrapped. And people say that they are saying thank you because of what Half-a-Ball-of-Kenki did for Fly long ago.

The Ashanti storyteller says: This is my story. If it be sweet, or if it be not sweet, take some and let the rest come back to me.